This igloo book belongs to:

....

Contents

Published in 2014
by Igloo Books Ltd
Cottage Farm
Sywell
NN6 0BJ
www.igloobooks.com

FIR003 1014
10 9 8 7 6 5 4 3 2 1
ISBN: 978-1-78440-174-0

Illustrated by Diane Le Feyer

Printed and manufactured in China

My 6-in-1 Treasury

Snow White
and other
Fairytales

igloobooks

Little Red Riding Hood

Once, there was a girl called Little Red Riding Hood whose granny lived in a deep, dark wood.

One day, Granny was ill, so Little Red Riding Hood took her a basket of cakes. "Don't talk to strangers," said her mother, as she waved goodbye.

In the wood, a hungry wolf stepped out. "Where are you going, little girl?" he asked. "I'm going to visit my granny," replied Little Red Riding Hood.

The wolf suggested that Little Red Riding Hood pick some flowers for her granny.

The hungry wolf wanted to eat Little Red Riding Hood and her granny. So, while she picked flowers, he crept away and ran to Granny's cottage as fast as he could. *Tap-tap*, he went on the door.

As soon as Granny answered, the wolf locked her in a cupboard. He put on her nightdress and cap and jumped into her bed, just in time to hear Little Red Riding Hood open the cottage door.

"Why, Granny," she said, "what big ears you have."
"All the better to hear you with," replied the wolf.
"Granny, what big eyes you have," said Little Red
Riding Hood, stepping closer. "All the better to see
you with," answered the wolf.

Little Red Riding Hood went right up to the bed. "Oh, Granny, what big teeth you have," she said.

Suddenly, the wolf threw back the covers and leapt out of bed. "All the better to EAT you with," he growled, licking his lips.

Outside, a woodcutter heard Little Red Riding Hood's cries and ran to help. "Go away, wolf and don't come back," he shouted.

The wolf took one look at the woodcutter's axe, gave a terrified howl and ran off into the wood.

Little Red Riding Hood and the woodcutter helped Granny out of the cupboard. Then, they all sat in the garden and had tea and cakes.

No one ever saw that nasty wolf again and after that, Little Red Riding Hood never talked to strangers again.

Hansel and Gretel

Long ago, a brother and sister, called Hansel and Gretel, lived with their woodcutter father and cruel stepmother. They were very poor and had no food to eat. "Take the children and leave them in the woods," said the stepmother.

The sad woodcutter led Hansel and Gretel into the woods. On the way, clever Hansel crumbled some bread and sprinkled a trail along the floor. "We shall follow this to find our way home," he whispered to his sister.

Alone in the woods, Hansel looked for the trail of
crumbs, but birds had eaten it. "I'm scared," said Gretel
and she began to cry. Suddenly, they came across a
cottage made from gingerbread and candy, with a
frosting roof sprinkled with sweets.

The children were so hungry, they broke off some gingerbread and ate it. No sooner had they done this than the cottage door opened and an old woman invited them in. Once they were inside, however, the woman, who was a witch, slammed the door.

The witch locked Hansel in a cage. Each day,
she felt Hansel's finger to see if it was plump, for she
meant to cook and eat him. Clever Hansel would hold
out a twig instead and the witch, who did not see well,
did not notice.

"Thin or fat, I shall cook you," said the witch. She ordered Gretel to creep into the oven to make sure there was plenty of room. Gretel said she needed the witch to show her how. So, the witch climbed into the oven and when she did, Gretel shoved her in and closed the door with a mighty slam.

Gretel freed Hansel from his cage. "We must run from this place," said Hansel, but first we shall find the witch's gold. So, the children searched the cottage and found the gold. "How will we find our way home?" asked Gretel. Just then, outside, a dove flew overhead.

The children followed the bird through the wood,
to their father's cottage. The woodcutter wept tears
of joy. "I was under your stepmother's spell," he said,
"but now she is gone forever."

So, Hansel and Gretel lived happily ever after
and never saw the wicked witch again.

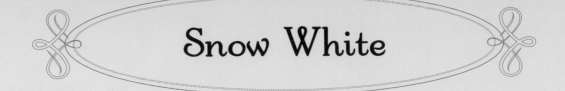

Snow White

Once, there was a princess called Snow White whose mother died. Snow White's stepmother was jealous of her and each day she asked her magic mirror exactly the same question. "Mirror, mirror, on the wall, who's the fairest of them all?"

"You are the fairest," replied the mirror.

One day, when the queen asked the question, the mirror replied, "Snow White is the fairest of them all." The queen was so angry that she ordered her huntsman to take Snow White into the woods and leave her there.

The huntsman left Snow White in the wood.
She wandered alone until she came to a little cottage.
Inside, was a table set with seven little plates and
seven knives and forks. Nearby were seven little beds.
Snow White was so tired, she laid down on one
and fell into a deep sleep.

Before long, there was a whistling sound outside. The door flew open and seven dwarves came in. They were very surprised to see Snow White, but when she told them her story, they said that she could stay. "We know all about that wicked queen," they said.

At the palace, the wicked queen said, "Mirror, mirror on the wall, who is the fairest of them all?"

"Snow White," replied the mirror. The queen was so angry, she dressed up as an old woman and set off into the wood. She found Snow White and gave her a poisoned apple.

Snow White bit the apple and fell to the floor.
The queen cackled and disappeared, just as the
dwarves returned. "Snow White is dead!" they
cried and they knew it must be the work of the
wicked queen.

Snow White lay in a glass coffin in the woods, watched over by the dwarves and the forest animals. Then, one day, a handsome prince rode by. As soon as he saw Snow White, the prince fell in love with her.

With one kiss the prince broke the queen's evil spell and Snow White woke up. Snow White fell in love with the prince and they were soon married.

The seven dwarves came to visit every day and no one was ever troubled by the wicked queen again.

Beauty and the Beast

Long ago, there was a girl called Beauty whose father was a poor merchant. One day, he went to the city to look for work. Beauty's sisters wanted him to bring them jewels, but Beauty asked only for a simple, pink rose.

The merchant did not find work, so he set off for home. On the way, he got lost in a vast wood. A storm blew and the merchant went to take shelter in a mysterious castle that was deep among the trees.

"Hello," he called, opening the door, but there was no reply. Inside, a delicious feast was laid out on a table, so the merchant sat down and ate, hungrily.

Afterwards, the merchant was tired, so he lay down and slept until morning.

As he left the next day, the merchant picked a pink rose for Beauty.

Suddenly, a snarling beast appeared. "Why have you picked my rose?" he roared. The merchant explained about Beauty. "I will let you go," growled the beast, "but you must send her to live with me."

The merchant went home and told Beauty about
the beast. So, she went to his castle to live with him.
The beast was kind to Beauty and gave her nice
clothes and jewels. Each night, they sat by the
firelight and talked.

"You are kind to me, Beast," said Beauty one day, "but I want to see my father." The beast gave Beauty a magic mirror to see him and an enchanted ring to bring her back the castle. "Make sure that you come back in seven days," he said.

Once she was home, Beauty decided to stay there. Then, one night, she looked in the mirror and saw the Beast howling in pain. She put on the ring and was suddenly back in the palace. "I love you, Beast," she sobbed, running to his side.

Magic sparkles flew around and the beast changed into a handsome man. "I am a prince who was cursed by an evil witch," he said. "Only true love could break the spell and make me human again."

Beauty and the prince were married and lived together happily ever after in their castle in the forest.

The Snow Queen

Long ago, a magician created a mirror that made whoever looked into it cold and cruel. One day, he dropped the mirror and it fell to Earth and smashed. Shards of the mirror flew on the wind to a small town where two friends called Gerda and Kay lived.

One winter evening, the friends were listening to a tale about the Snow Queen, whose icy touch would freeze the warmest heart. Kay looked up to the sky and laughed at such a silly story. It was then that a tiny splinter of the magician's mirror fell into his eye and another pierced his heart.

Kay became cold and cruel. He ignored Gerda and played with other boys.

Then, one day, a glittering sledge swept into the town and in it was a woman who wore a cape made entirely from snow, for she was the Snow Queen. She wrapped Kay in her icy embrace and carried him away, over the frozen river.

When spring came, Gerda set off in a little boat to
find Kay. The river carried her until the boat came
to rest by a little cottage where an old woman lived.
The woman gave Gerda enchanted cherries which
made her forget Kay, until a magic flower told Gerda
that Kay was still alive.

Gerda ran far into the forest where she found a prince and princess in a palace. They took pity on her and gave her clothes and a carriage. Once again, Gerda set off to find Kay, but a band of robbers took her prisoner.

A little robber girl felt sorry for Gerda. "Take my reindeer and go North," she said. "Find the Finland woman and she will tell you of the Snow Queen."

In the North, the Finland woman gave Gerda a magic potion. "Now you will travel to the palace of the Snow Queen," said the woman.

In a spiral of light, Gerda arrived at the vast, frozen palace. There she found Kay, lifeless and cold. Gerda's bitter tears trickled onto Kay's icy skin and the splinters in his eye and heart washed away.

Kay woke and hugged his beloved friend. The Snow Queen watched, her eyes like cold fire. "The strength of your love is no match for me," she said and she disappeared in a spiral of snowflakes, leaving Kay and Gerda to return safely home.

The Frog Prince

One day, a little princess was playing with her golden ball when it fell, PLOP! into the palace pond. "Oh, no!" she cried, peering into the deep water. "I'll get your ball," croaked a little frog, "if you let me eat from your plate, sleep on your pillow and give me a kiss."

The princess had no intention of kissing an ugly frog, but she wanted her ball back, so she agreed. The frog dived into the water and came back with the golden ball. The princess snatched it and quickly ran away without another word.

That evening, however, the frog came to the palace to claim his kiss.

"Have you forgotten your promise?" the frog asked the princess, hopping into the banqueting hall. "If you have made a promise, you must keep it," said the king to the princess.

So, the frog slurped from the princess's cup and snatched food from her plate with his long, pink tongue. "Urgh!" said the princess, looking disgusted.

When it was time for bed, the princess carried the
frog to her bedroom, where he snored all night long.

In the morning, he asked for his kiss. "You are
slimy and disgusting," said the princess, "but I will at
last be rid of you." So, she kissed the frog.

Suddenly, there was a flash of sparkling light and the frog transformed into a handsome prince. "I was under the spell of a witch," he explained, smiling, "but now you have set me free."

The prince and the princess fell in love and the princess was always glad that, in the end, she had kept her promise and kissed a frog.